Danny Boyle and the Ghosts of Ireland

Copyright © 2002 William Graham
All rights reserved.

No part of this book may be reproduced, stored in a retrieval system, or transmitted by any means, electronic, mechanical, photocopying, recording, or otherwise, without written permission from the author.

ISBN 1-58898-693-4

Danny Boyle and the Ghosts of Ireland

William Graham

greatunpublished.com
Title No.693
2002

Danny Boyle and the Ghosts of Ireland

To Jacqueline and the Metaphor that is Ireland

Chapter 1

Kevin Flynn saw someone dash across the road in front of him as he was heading home late in the evening from his job as bartender at Vaughan's Pub in Lisdoonvarna, Country Clare, Ireland. He slammed on the breaks and got out of his car to look around. He saw nothing in the car's headlights. Yet he was convinced that he saw a man carrying golf clubs run across the road right in front of his car. But why would anyone be out here on a cold and rainy night with golf clubs, he thought to himself. Flynn decided that he should stop having so many beers while he worked. He continued on down the narrow road to his small house. "Better to not mention anything to the wife," he mumbled as he stepped out of his car and rushed through his front door to escape the rain that had become heavier.

People all around Lisdoonvarna were scratching their heads and checking their eyesight on this night, for the local ghosts were gathering for their weekly meeting to swap stories and plan new games to scare "the breathers," which is how they referred to human beings.

Flynn had seen the spirit of Brendan Connelly, whose regular haunt was the locker room and the fifteenth tee of Doogan's Cross Golf and Croquet Club. He haunted the fifteenth tee because that was where he was struck by lightning fifty years ago when he was up two strokes on his golfing rival Billy McLain. Humans think that ghosts just haunt old musty castles and graveyards. But that's not true. You can find a ghost almost anywhere.

All the local ghosts showed up at one minute past midnight

on Sunday mornings. They wouldn't miss this chance to socialize because being a ghost was often a lonely occupation.

Joining Brendan was Molly O'Meara, who scared young girls at Flatley's College Preparatory School in Kilfenora. Patrick Byrne also was a regular. Patrick lurked in the back rows of local movie houses and sat on people's laps during scary movies.

Sean McKenna floated briskly over the limestone rocks in the damp, dark fields to join the group. Sean's specialty was stealing the hats from tourists who stayed in small hotels. His ghost friends asked him why he needed so many hats. He replied: "Oh, I never use the hats. I'm a bloody ghost. It's just the sport I enjoy." Sean always returned the hats, much to the relief of the people who had thought they had lost them. Dozens of other ghosts joined Brendan, Molly, Patrick and Sean in the field near an ancient Celtic burial site.

There was also one invited guest: Owen Kildare. He was known as Killer Kildare because he had murdered two people who had worked in a bank. His spirit had an eerie red tint to it because he had blood on his hands when he was alive. While living and as a spirit, however, Owen just wanted to be liked. But he never had been able to fit in or to make friends. As a human being, he turned to crime to make himself feel important. As a ghost, he aligned himself with the evil spirits because they would take him in.

"Go away, Owen. You're not welcome here," Molly said as she and her ghost friends floated above the field.

"I'm a ghost. I can go anywhere I want to," Owen replied. "What are you talking about?"

"You know what we're talking about," Sean said. "New and fun ways to scare the breathers."

"What you come up with is always boring," Owen replied.

"Then just go," Sean said. The other ghosts began chanting: "Go away, Killer Kildare."

"What if I were to tell you that something big is brewing among the ghost council in the north," said Owen.

"You mean the dark council of Dermot McCullough?"

Molly said. "We're not interested in what Dermot the Daring has to say."

"I think you should. But I'm not going to tell you because you haven't been very neighborly," Owen said.

"You don't know what neighborly means," Brendan said as he waved one of his golf clubs through Owen as he floated there.

"Fine," Owen said as he elevated himself above the others and soared into the dark sky. "But now you'll pay the price. Go ahead and stay here and play your childish games. The real power of the spirit world is Dermot McCullough!"

"Then go pay homage to the great Dermot. We have better things to do," Patrick said.

Owen left the ghosts hovering in the field. He had been shunned again. He departed angry and lonely.

Throughout the night, the ghosts of Lisdoonvarna shared stories, laughed and made plans for more ways to scare human as they always did. At first light, the field was damp and silent except for the bleating of sheep and the muted roar of the Atlantic Ocean pounding against the steep cliffs nearby. The ghosts were gone from sight, but they were always around. They could perform their ghostly deeds during the day, but they much preferred the night when they could scare people even more.

Chapter 2

Danny Boyle had a map of Ireland spread out on his bed. He was carefully circling all of the destinations where he and his family would be going on their summer vacation. He had circled Dublin, County Wicklow, Galway and other places with magical names like Connemara, Killarney and Lisdoonvarna. Danny carefully traced his fingers across the map like it was a piece of treasure.

His parents, his sister Melinda and he were going to spend three weeks in the land of his ancestors. His father called Ireland the "old sod" because of the abundance of turf in Ireland that people still used as fuel to heat their homes. Danny loved to read about distant locations, but this was the first time that he would be getting on a plane and traveling to a place that he had only read about or had stared at on a map. He was twelve years old. He figured he had been waiting long enough.

Danny lived in Rivertown, a small community perched high on a bluff above the Mississippi River. Not much happened in Rivertown, so Danny was always looking for adventure wherever he could find it. And his best friend Chip Zumhoffer was usually along for the search. Chip, however, would not be joining Danny in Ireland. Chip was heading to Wisconsin for a three-week baseball camp. Danny, like Chip, loved baseball, especially the hometown team the Rivertown Roughnecks. But as tantalizing as a baseball camp was, it was not Ireland. Ireland was far away. With all due respect to Wisconsin, Ireland was a foreign country, and that made all the difference to Danny.

Danny's map gazing was interrupted by an explosion of curly red hair and waving arms, otherwise know as his ten-year-old sister Melinda. Even though Danny was two years older than Melinda, they were in the same grade. This fact annoyed Danny and brought heaps of joy to Melinda, who told everyone she met that she had jumped ahead two grades because she was special.

"Are you still staring at that old map? I've been doing something practical," Melinda said.

"Go away," Danny said, keeping his eyes down on the map.

"Don't you want to know what I've been doing?"

"Does it look like it?"

"Well, I'll tell you anyway. I've been learning some words in the native Irish language," Melinda said proudly.

"But people in Ireland speak English," Danny reminded her.

"Here's one. In Irish, Ireland is called Eire. A river is known as "abhainn." It's pronounced 'owan', however," Melinda said, ignoring Danny's response completely.

"Well, you can talk to the leprechauns there," Danny said.

"There are no such things as leprechauns. They're just a legend. You know, something that isn't real," Melinda said.

"I know what a legend is," Danny said. "But there are some dark and mysterious places in Ireland that I want to explore. You never know what you might find."

"We'll go wherever Mom and Dad take us," Melinda said. "And that's that."

"Yeah, yeah," Danny said. "Now can I go back to what I was doing?"

"Fine. I'm going to learn more words and begin packing," Melinda said as she whirled around and headed down the hall to her room.

Danny had already packed. Even though it was summer, Ireland can be cool and damp, so he had packed a rain jacket and pants and his waterproof hiking shoes that his parents had given him for his last birthday. He then packed a copy of *A Boy's Guide to Baseball History* to read on the long plane ride. Finally, he placed his Rivertown Roughnecks baseball hat on top of his backpack so that he could take a little piece of Rivertown baseball tradition with him on his journey.

Danny didn't sleep well the night before he and his family went to the airport. He dreamed that he was alone on a windy island surrounded by floating balls of light that were leading him to the edge of a cliff. He then began falling down toward the boiling ocean below. Just as he was about to hit the rocks at the bottom of the cliff, he heard his mother telling him to wake up because it was time to get ready. His adventure in Ireland was about to begin.

Chapter 3

As Danny and his family were flying through the dark skies above the Atlantic Ocean toward Dublin, Dermot the Daring and his ghostly disciples were gathering in the post-midnight gloom of the Black Fort on the island of Inishmore. The ruined fort was perched on a precariously steep cliff. The murky Atlantic Ocean bellowed more than three hundred feet below the broken battlements.

Dermot had been a spirit for over one thousand years. He had a huge head with tangled black hair and a scruffy beard. He hovered through the air wearing fur robes and an angry scowl on his face that could turn the blood of friend and foe alike cold. He died fighting against the Vikings in the legendary Battle of Clontarf in the year 1014. In his time, he was known as a brave but ruthless leader, who would betray anyone to succeed. But he also inspired loyalty. Through the centuries, he had persuaded many spirits to join his dark council. And through the centuries, Dermot and his followers scared many human beings and haunted many castles and graveyards.

They particularly liked to frighten widows who were visiting the graves of their dear departed husbands. On one occasion, while a widow named Nell Breslin was placing flowers and saying a prayer at the foot of her husband John's grave, Dermot pretended to be the voice of John. He told Nell all kinds of mean things. Then he lifted Nell into the sky and placed her in a branch of a tall tree in the graveyard. Nell yelled hysterically, until the grave keeper rescued her with a ladder. Dermot laughed sarcastically. Thereafter, Nell sent her son David to the graveyard.

But now Dermot wanted to do something more than just scare the old widows and other breathers. He wanted to create an army of spirits to wage war on human beings.

As hundreds of ghosts floated above the broken and scattered stones of the Black Fort, Dermot explained his dark plan.

"The breathers have taken over Ireland. But this land belongs to us. We should be ruling the humans, not just scaring them. Many of the humans don't even believe in us. They mock us. They even pretend to be of the spirit world and dress up as ghosts and goblins and witches. But we will not be mocked!"

"We must revive the master plan of the great Padraic the Pale. We must enter the bodies of the breathers and make them do our bidding. That is our noble plan. We will bring the breathers to their knees and we will control the land of our fathers. They won't even know what is happening," Dermot said.

The other ghosts were silent. They knew what Dermot's ideas meant—a war between Dermot's forces and the good spirits who merely wanted to play with human beings, not destroy them or their world.

"Dermot," said the ghost named Brian, "are you aware of what this means?"

"Of course, it means a battle will be fought. It's a battle we will win!" Dermot responded, raising his clenched fist and shaking his hairy head violently.

"Everyone here should be aware of the possible consequences," Brian said.

"What consequences?" Owen Kildare said. Owen only wanted to fight if he knew what the outcome would be in advance. Even though Owen had an evil reputation, he was actually scared of difficult confrontations where the outcome might be in doubt.

"Will you tell him, Dermot, or should I?" Brian said.

"Owen, my friend, " Dermot said. "And everyone gathered here tonight. The price of failure is being eternally banned to the Forest of Kenmare by the spirits of light—the good spirits as they call themselves. You will be forever entombed in the trees to groan with the strong winds, weep with the rains and crack from the cold for all eternity. But we will not lose. We cannot lose. Are you all with me?"

For a moment there was silence as the ghosts pondered what Dermot had told them. In victory there would be power. In defeat there would be banishment. The ghosts of the dark council all feared Dermot and, even if they had doubts, they told themselves that Dermot could not be wrong and that he could not be defeated.

Chapter 4

Danny, Melinda and their parents arrived in Dublin—the capital city of Ireland—on a cold, rainy day in June. As the plane descended through the clouds, Danny pressed his face against the window and gazed at the deep green fields of Ireland. It was the deepest green he had ever seen. Danny could barely contain his enthusiasm.

Danny and his family were staying in an old hotel called Baggot's near Trinity College, which was near a large city park called St. Stephen's Green. Even though they were excited about being in a place so far away from home, Danny and Melinda were also exhausted by the long flight.

But after a brief nap and a change of clothes, Danny was ready to explore the old hotel and the surrounding neighborhood.

His parents told him to wait for them in the lobby while they and Melinda checked with the hotel staff for walking tours around Dublin. Danny sat in the grand lobby that had high ceilings like a church and glowing crystal chandeliers. The dark wooden walls seemed to embrace the room. A huge, warm fire burned and crackled in the ornate fireplace.

As Danny sat in a large leather chair near the fire, he noticed that the small tables near the chairs began to move across the floor. He was startled. He thought that he might still be tired after all. He took off his glasses and rubbed his eyes.

After checking his eyesight, the tables stopped moving. Danny felt better. He was calm once again. But then the tables moved for a second time. Danny swiveled his head around to see if anybody else had noticed the tables moving. Neither the other guests nor the hotel staff were paying any attention to the furniture.

Then the crystal chandeliers hanging from the ceiling began to sway, as if there was an earthquake. But there are no earthquakes in Ireland, Danny thought. And then the strangest thing of all happened: Danny began to shiver with cold even though he was sitting in front of a roaring fire. He felt as if a hand of ice was poking him in the ribs.

Just as he was about to get up from the chair to call to his parents, he heard a voice whisper in his ear. "Follow me," the voice said.

"Who's there?" Danny said.

"Follow me," the voice said again.

Danny loved adventure, or at least reading about adventure. But there was definitely something happening to him that he hadn't read about in any books. Danny glanced at Melinda and his parents, who were still talking to the hotel staff at the front desk.

He decided to follow the voice. He couldn't help himself.

"This way," it said again.

The voice directed him down a twisting hallway to a door to a large ballroom. A sign on the door read: "Keep Out. Under Renovation."

As Danny approached the door, it slowly creaked open, revealing a large empty ballroom that had scaffolds and paint cans and other construction equipment scattered on the floor.

It was dark. Danny was trying to adjust his eyes to the darkness when a figure of a man dressed in a tuxedo floated in front of him. But Danny realized that it wasn't a real man, but a ghost. Then Danny saw another ghost with a bald head and rosy cheeks. The ghost was dressed elegantly with a white flower in his lapel. The ghost was holding the hand of a woman with blond hair piled on her head. She wore a stunning black gown with small pointed shoes. The entire ballroom was filled with well-dressed ghosts dancing near the ceiling. There was no sound, however. There was no orchestra playing music. But the ghosts were waltzing anyway in their tuxedos, gowns and shiny shoes, as if they were still alive.

"Welcome to Baggot's Hotel," said one ghost who was wearing a bright red rose in his jacket. "We always like to do something special for selected first-time visitors to our quaint establishment. But don't let us frighten you. You were chosen from among all of the guests to see our little party."

"Why me?" Danny asked. He could barely speak this simple sentence. He tried to remain calm, but his knees were shaking and his mouth was dry.

"Because you look like a young man who appreciates things, shall we say, out of the ordinary," the ghost said.

"Can other people see you?"

"Only if we want them to. But you have to go now. I hear a little girl with a large voice calling your name."

"That's my sister Melinda."

"Her voice could wake the dead!" said the ghost. All of the other ghosts laughed and resumed their swirling dance.

Danny returned to the lobby to meet his parents and Melinda's scowling face. He mentioned nothing about the dancing ghosts to anyone.

Chapter 5

Danny and Melinda and their parents spent the day acting like typical tourists. The joined a walking tour of Dublin and learned about its history—from the time of the ancient Celts, who were the distant ancestors of today's Irish people—to the more recent events. They visited nearby Trinity College and saw the treasures in its library. They also spent most of the afternoon in the National Museum where they learned about ancient Ireland and saw gleaming gold chalices, gigantic swords and other menacing battle gear.

For most of the day, Danny acted as if nothing had happened. He tried to forget the ghosts that he had seen dancing at Baggot's Hotel. He diverted his thoughts to enjoying the sights as he walked through the narrow streets that were gleaming now that the sun had broken through the low clouds. He loved gazing at the old buildings and learning about the history of the city and of Ireland. He even tolerated Melinda's regular translations of Irish words into English. His parents thought that she was being charming. Danny thought otherwise, but he had learned to keep the peace by keeping quiet.

As he and his family were strolling along Grafton Street looking at wool sweaters in a shop window, Danny stopped suddenly and gasped. Ahead, hovering above the crowd, was the ghost with the red rose in its lapel—the same ghost to whom he had spoken in the old ballroom. The ghost waved at Danny as if he were greeting him casually as an old friend. Then the next moment the ghost disappeared.

"What are you staring at?" Melinda said.

"What?" Danny said. "Oh, nothing. I'm just getting hungry. Can we stop someplace and eat?"

Melinda and his parents thought that Danny was being unusually quiet during dinner.

"I'm still a bit tired from the long trip I guess," Danny explained.

Melinda, however, kept the dinner conversation lively with her vigorous complaining that the fish was dry and that the vegetables and chips were boring.

"We didn't come here for the great food, dear," her mother told her. "We came here for the beauty of the land and the great culture."

"That's the truth," Melinda scowled as she pushed her unfinished food away from her.

After dinner, Danny's parents went to their hotel room, while Melinda and Danny went to theirs, which was next door. They were both excited about having their own hotel room, even though they had to share it with each other. "Just don't kill each other," Danny's mother told them before they went to bed.

The last rays of light dripped through the curtains at ten o'clock at night because summer days in Ireland are long and the nights are short. In the distance Danny could hear the faint sounds of Irish folk music being played at a nearby pub. Melinda wasn't tired, however. She was trying to find something interesting to watch on television.

"Can't you find a station and leave it on for more than ten seconds?" Danny said.

"I'm trying to find something I like. The shows and channels are different here," Melinda said as she continued to press the buttons on the remote control with growing speed and frustration while sitting on the edge of her bed.

As Danny watched her fly through the different TV channels, he decided that he needed to talk to her about ghosts. He couldn't keep his secret any longer.

"Do you believe in ghosts?" Danny asked suddenly.

"What? Ghosts? There's no such thing," Melinda said confidently. "That's a stupid question."

"How do you know for sure?" Danny said, ignoring Melinda's snide remark.

"Because they're just silly legends."

Danny was getting angry at Melinda's combative attitude. He decided to drop a big bomb on her snooty confidence.

"Oh, yeah. Well, I saw a ghost today. In fact, I saw dozens of ghosts right here in this hotel," Danny said.

"No you didn't," Melinda replied swiftly, as she continued to flip through the TV channels.

"Yes I did. Remember when you couldn't find me in the lobby this morning? I left because I was asked by a ghost to follow him to an old ballroom that's being fixed up. The ghosts were there, and they were dancing. This hotel is haunted by ghosts," Danny said, knowing that what he had just confessed would make him sound a little crazy.

"I can't believe you're telling me this. I don't believe you. You're trying to scare me. But I don't believe you. Now let me watch TV," Melinda said.

"I'll prove it to you if you come to the ballroom with me," Danny said.

"No way. I'm in my pajamas, and it's late. Besides, if there are ghosts here, why weren't you scared? Ghosts are supposed to be scary. They try to frighten people, don't they?" Melinda said.

"These ghosts weren't like that. They weren't frightening. In fact, they welcomed me," Danny said.

"Now I really don't believe you," Melinda said. "I'm going to tell Mom and Dad that you're trying to scare me with ghost stories."

"Don't!" Danny yelled. "If we go to the ballroom early tomorrow before breakfast and the ghosts are there, will you believe me then? Come with me if you're so sure they won't be there."

"OK. Fine, " Melinda said. "If that's what it takes to prove you wrong, I'll come. I'm not scared of something that doesn't exist."

"Good," Danny said, pulling the covers over his head in his bed. "How much longer are you going to watch TV?"

"As long as I feel like it," Melinda said.

This vacation is off to a great start, Danny thought as he burrowed under the covers and tried to fall asleep. At times like these, Danny wished that he had stayed an only child. The most miserable day of his life was when his parents pushed a tiny red, crying bundle in his face and told him: "Look, you're a big brother now!" There has been nothing but aggravation since, he thought as he pulled his pillow over his head.

Chapter 6

Danny and Melinda crept down the empty stairs of Baggot's Hotel before six o'clock in the morning, long before their parents would be awake. They stopped in the lobby to see if anyone was there. But it was empty except for the night clerk who was sleeping behind the long marble desk.

Danny instructed Melinda to follow him to the hallway that led to the old ballroom. Just as they were turning a corner, they ran into a hotel maid. Her gray hair was pulled tight on her head in a bun. And her chin drooped almost to her chest.

"Can I help you two?" the woman said.

"We're heading to the restaurant for breakfast," Melinda said.

"Breakfast won't be served until six-thirty. Are ya by yourselves? And where might your parents be?" the woman inquired. Her fleshy chin wiggled as she spoke. Her Irish accent was so thick that Danny and Melinda had difficulty understanding her.

"They're still asleep. But they trust us. We're very responsible," said Melinda, after figuring out what the woman had asked them.

"Responsible, are ya now," she said. "Maybe I should be ringing your parents' room now and see what they have to say."

"No don't," Danny pleaded. Before he could speak another word, Melinda chimed in.

"Actually, we're here because my brother thinks that there are ghosts dancing in the old ballroom down the hall," Melinda said.

"Melinda!" Danny said as his face turned red.

"Ghosts, do ya say," the woman replied.

"That's right. Here in the hotel. Do you think there are ghosts here?" Melinda said.

"Well," the maid said, lowering her voice to a whisper. "I probably shouldn't be telling ya this, but other guests have been making complaints through the years about some strange noises and visions ever since the accident."

"What accident?" Danny asked.

"The fire in the grand ballroom a good thirty years ago now. Over forty people died. It was a terrible tragedy. God rest their souls," the maid said as she made the sign of the cross on her chest.

"Have you seen any ghosts?" Melinda asked.

"No, miss," she said. "But sometimes I do feel a chill when I walk too close to the ballroom. The hotel manager fixes it up year after year, but plaster starts falling and paint begins peeling off the walls almost as soon as it's put up. And the workmen complain that their tools suddenly disappear. It's the strangest thing. It's hard to find anyone who will work in that old ballroom anymore. So now you stay away from that old ballroom. It's no place for little ones. Get back to your room before I call your parents. I'm not telling ya again!"

The maid pushed Danny and Melinda out of the hallway and back up the stairs. They waited inside their room until the maid had left. Then they dashed back down the stairs and to the entrance to the ballroom. The large double doors were locked.

"Well, open the door and show me the ghosts, if there are any ghosts," Melinda said.

"It's locked," Danny said, as he pushed his right shoulder against the doors.

"Push it harder," Melinda ordered.

"Who made you the boss?" Danny said.

"Just push. Here, I'll help."

They both leaned against the doors with all of their weight. The doors slowly opened into the darkened ballroom, which was completely empty.

"I don't see anything," Melinda said. "I knew it."

Just then the ghost to whom Danny had spoken appeared.

"Is she safe?" the ghost inquired.

"She's my sister Melinda. She doesn't believe you exist," Danny said.

"Who are you talking to?" Melinda said.

"To me, little red-haired lass. Liam O'Rourke at your service," the ghost said, bowing like a gentleman before Melinda.

Melinda screamed and started running toward the doors, which closed with a bang, locking her and Danny in.

"Hey, let me out!" Melinda began screaming, as she pounded on the doors.

"Mr. Boyle, please control your sister," said the ghost named Liam.

"Melinda, please be quiet. Liam won't hurt you. Will you Liam?" Danny said.

"I'm not one of those kind of ghosts. I have a good reputation to uphold," Liam said.

"You hear that, Melinda? Just calm down," Danny said.

Melinda whirled around and pointed a finger at Liam: "You shouldn't scare people like that."

"Please accept my deepest apologies, Miss Boyle," Liam said.

"You see. There are ghosts. They are real," Danny said.

"Fine. Let's go. I won't tell anybody," Melinda said. "Hey, wait a minute. How do you know our names?"

"I always make it a point to know the names of all the guests at Baggot's, whether I decide to haunt their room or not. Any more questions, Miss Boyle?"

"That's all for now. But I'll have some more. I'm just letting you know ahead of time that I probably will," Melinda said.

"Now let me ask a question," Danny said. "Did you die in the fire here thirty years ago. One of the maids told us this story."

"Yes, Mr. Boyle. I did die in that tragic blaze, as did dozens of others. We were all enjoying ourselves on a Saturday night. The music was wonderful. So when we became spirits, we decided to stay here and relive the moments before the blaze for all eternity. The moments when we were dancing and laughing and singing," Liam said.

"But where are the others? I don't hear any music," Melinda said.

"Oh, Miss Boyle, there is no music except for the music that we hear in our world. And as for the others, they are taking a break. You get tired dancing for eternity."

"Why did you appear to Danny?" Melinda asked. "You see, I told you that I would have more questions."

"Does young Miss Boyle always ask so many questions?" Liam said.

"Yes, she does," Danny said.

"My teachers tell me it's important to ask questions," Melinda said.

"So it is, Miss Boyle. So it is," Liam said, smiling.

"I appeared to Mr. Boyle because every so often we sense a person who is not afraid of our spirit form. A person who is not afraid of ghosts and a little adventure. And we sometimes like to talk with breathers. Just talking to fellow ghosts can get awfully dull."

"Breathers?" Danny said.

"Live human beings such as you two, " Liam explained. "So are you glad I introduced myself to you, Mr. Boyle?"

"You bet. I do like a good adventure. You're right about that. And talking to a ghost is pretty cool. It doesn't happen everyday," Danny said.

"And you, Miss Boyle? Are you glad?"

"I guess it's kind of interesting. But don't go scaring people who might not want to see you," Melinda said.

"I wouldn't think of it, Miss Boyle. All I ask is that you keep this a secret. We don't want to cause any trouble for the Baggot's Hotel. We like it here."

"We won't tell, will we, Melinda?" Danny said.

"No, I promise," Melinda said.

"Well, then, I suggest that you return to your room and

enjoy breakfast with your parents. The eggs are particularly good here," Liam said as he faded away.

Danny and Melinda returned to their room and got dressed. Their parents had no idea what Danny and Melinda had seen. Danny and Melinda knew how to keep secrets.

Chapter 7

From Carndonagh in the north to Clonakilty in the south, and from Wicklow in the east to Dingle in the west, Dermot the Daring began recruiting evil ghosts to his dark council. All across the island of Ireland, ghosts who had been haunting graveyards and churches, castles and schools, homes and bus stations with malicious intent were now drawn into Dermot's army of spirits.

Ghosts who had once been powerful in the real world would now rule again, according to Dermot, who said he knew where the lost chalice of the Celts was hidden. This chalice would allow the spirits to control all human beings because spirits would be able to enter the bodies of the breathers and control their thoughts and actions.

"You will continue to be immortal, but you will have the power to change events in the world of the breathers, the world from where we all came," Dermot boasted. This promise appealed to many ghosts who were bored with their routine existence in the spirit world. Now, with Dermot, they could experience some real action once again.

Dermot took his army to a cave deep in the Macgillycuddy Mountains. Hundreds of spirits entered an underground chamber where they gazed on the golden chalice, from which the kings of the ancient Celts once drank. A Celtic priest named Boru had given the chalice its powerful properties.

Dermot instructed the ghosts to touch the chalice with their icy fingers. With once touch, the ghosts would be able to control the minds and bodies of human beings.

At once, things began to change mysteriously in Ireland.

The ghosts of children who were picked on when they were alive now entered the bodies of children who were afraid of bullies. With the ghostly power now in them, these same children fought back and the bullies became afraid of them. The ghosts of politicians who had lost elections entered the bodies of mayors and senators and began changing the laws throughout the country. Ghosts who were poor athletes entered the bodies of powerful Irish football players. Ghosts of mothers who had lost their children in car accidents or to diseases entered the bodies of mothers who had large families so that they could feel what it was like to hug a son or daughter again.

Owen "Killer" Kildare entered the body of a jail warden and released all of the robbers and murderers. Dermot the Daring entered the body of the prime minister who ruled Ireland. Dermot's closest ghost associates entered the bodies of the other ministers, judges and leading politicians.

Dermot couldn't have been happier. He was in charge again. People were once again bowing to his orders. His plan was working. Ireland was now in his hands, where it should have been one thousand years ago, he thought. In just a few days, he had turned Ireland upside down.

Dermot was also showing his true side to the dark council. He would not listen to one of the members of the council to whom he had promised so much. He declared himself the supreme ruler of the living and the dead. He mocked all those around him, especially Owen.

"You're a little vermin, Owen Kildare—a rat, a bug, a piece of lice. While you were living, you killed only two people. I killed hundreds of foes in glorious battles. You, like the others, are nothing compared to me. I don't even know why I recruited you in the first place," Dermot said.

Owen said nothing, nor did the other members of the dark council. Once powerful and evil in their lifetimes, they quaked at the sight and sound of Dermot. They dared not cross him as he charted his evil course. And his evil plan was working all too well.

The citizens of Ireland began noticing changes in the

behavior of people whom they had known all of their lives, but no one could figure out exactly what was going on. Ireland was in turmoil. The spirit world was in turmoil. Ghosts like Brendan Connelly who opposed Dermot looked for a way to stop what was going on. He heard from his friend Liam O'Rourke about two American children who were staying at Baggot's Hotel. Brendan then knew what he had to do.

Chapter 8

Brendan traveled swiftly—for ghosts can get from one place to another in just a few seconds—to Doreen Cavanaugh's small cottage near Lisdoonvarna. The ghosts knew that Doreen was a witch because she had the power to make things in the real world appear and disappear. But Doreen's neighbors just thought she was weird because she spoke to herself and howled like a dog when she went out at nights in the empty fields. Everyone called her Demented Doreen. Doreen didn't care, however. She liked her quiet life in the stone cottage sitting by the roaring fire, making potions in her copper cauldron and conversing with spirits.

Doreen was reading a chapter in the book *Do-It-Yourself Curses* when Brendan appeared above the mantel of her fireplace.

"Brendan, so nice to see you," Doreen said, placing the book on a table next to her leather chair. Her cat Merlin yawned and went back to sleep. "What's the occasion?"

"You've been hearing about the strange things that have been happening all around the country?" Brendan said.

"Oh, yes," Doreen said. "But I pay the newspapers no mind. You can't trust politicians and other people who don't have magical powers."

"It's serious. Very serious," Brendan said as he floated down to sit in a chair next to Doreen's. "Dermot the Daring has found the golden chalice of Boru. He and his dark council have invaded the bodies of the breathers. Dermot is now ruling Ireland."

"That can't be," Doreen said. "The Celtic chalice was supposed to be hidden forever."

"Well, Dermot has found it."

"My, my. This is serious indeed."

"You know what we must do?"

"Yes. The legend says that we have to find two pure and brave souls from a distant land who will gather a group of ancient relics whose power will overcome that of the golden chalice," Doreen said.

"And with the power of the chalice gone, Dermot and his dark council will be banished for eternity in the Forest of Kenmare."

"But where will be find such people?" Doreen asked.

"I believe that I have found them. Two American children whom my friend Liam O'Rourke met at Baggot's," Brendan said.

"They weren't scared of Liam?"

"No."

"They can't be traveling alone, can they?" Doreen asked.

"No, they are with their parents. That's why I came here to visit, Doreen. We need you to create their doubles so that their parents won't know that they're missing, that they're working with us against Dermot," Brendan said.

"But the plan will fail if the children don't agree. They must be willing participants," Doreen said.

"I believe they will help us," Brendan said. "I trust Liam's judgement in these matters."

"We must hurry then. I've got my wand and doppelgänger dust in a bag somewhere. I'll meet you at Baggot's. What room?"

"Room 312," Brendan said. "I'll also bring Liam."

In room 312 of Baggot's Hotel, Danny and Melinda were sleeping quietly, unaware of what Brendan and Doreen were planning. Danny and Melinda's parents had decided to shorten their trip because of the sudden turmoil in Ireland. Danny and Melinda protested. They were having a great time seeing all of the wonderful places like old castles and graveyards. But they were scheduled to leave on a flight back to Rivertown tomorrow morning.

Danny was tossing and turning in his bed. He always did this when he was in the middle of an exciting dream. At the moment, he was dreaming about fighting a giant.

He heard someone whispering in his ear. He thought that he was still dreaming, but then he awoke and saw Liam hovering over his bed.

"Liam, what are you doing here?" Danny asked, rubbing the sleep out of his eyes.

"I brought some friends who want to speak with you and Miss Boyle," Liam explained.

Out of the shadows stepped Brendan and Doreen.

"Let me introduce my friend Brendan Connelly. He's a ghost of course. And Doreen Cavanaugh. But she's a breather like you. She's also a witch," Liam said.

"A witch? Where?" Melinda said, rising up from under the covers.

"I thought you were sleeping," Danny said.

"How can a girl sleep with all of this racket," Melinda said. "You don't look like a witch. You're kind of pretty."

Doreen was not dressed in a black robe and she did not wear a pointed black hat. Those are the kind of witches that you read about in fairy tales. Doreen was dressed in blue jeans, a red sweater and a shawl. She had strawberry blond hair and large green eyes. She was carrying her wand a large brown bag.

"Thank you, miss," Doreen said. "I don't look too bad if I do say so myself."

"Enough chit-chat," Brendan said. "Remember that we're here on important business."

"What do you mean?" Danny said.

"You've heard about all of the bizarre things that are happening in our country," Brendan said.

"Yes," Danny replied. "That's why our parents told us that we leave tomorrow, even though we don't want to go."

"We like it here," Melinda said.

"What if you didn't have to leave tomorrow?" Doreen inquired.

"But we have to," Melinda said.

"Not if I create your exact twins, also known as doppengängers," Doreen said.

"I've read about doppelgängers," Melinda said proudly. "Doppelgängers are exact doubles of a living person."

"You're a smart young lass," Doreen said.

"Don't encourage her," Danny said.

"We're here to create your exact doubles so that you can stay here in Ireland. Your parents will think that you are going back to America with them," Brendan said.

"Will our doppelgängers sound and act like us as well?" Danny asked.

"Of course. That's why I'm a great witch," Doreen said. "And when your mission is over, we'll take you back to your home and the doppelgängers will disappear. Everything will be perfect."

"Our mission? What mission? What's going on?" Melinda said.

"Uh, you see young lad and lass," Brendan said. "We can fix it so you'll stay in Ireland a wee bit longer if you help us fight Dermot the Daring."

"Who?" Danny said.

"You see," Liam said. "Dermot the Daring is a bad ghost, a black spirit. He and his dark council have invaded the bodies of many powerful people here in Ireland. It's the ghosts who are causing all of the troubles. They weren't content, like we are, just to scare a few people from time to time. They want to rule people. They got hold of the golden Celtic chalice, which gave them the power to take over people's minds and bodies. The only way that the spell can be broken is if we find two pure and brave souls from a distant land who can gather other relics from around Ireland to break the power of the chalice."

"And we thought of you two," Brendan said. "If you want to help us. We're not forcing you now. You can go home tomorrow if you want."

"Will it be dangerous?" Melinda asked.

"Maybe a wee bit," Brendan said. "But it will be a grand adventure."

"An adventure, Melinda. I'm in," Danny said. "How about you?"

"I don't know, Danny, " Melinda said.

"Come on," Danny said. "I'll probably need your help from time to time."

"That's true," Melinda said. "OK. I'll do it, but only if Doreen can really make good doppelgängers. We don't want to scare Mom and Dad."

"You can count on me, lass," Doreen said. "Just watch me.

Doreen tossed grey, sparkling dust from her bag over Melinda and Danny. Then she spoke an ancient Irish incantation as she waved her wand around their bodies. There was a flash of light. The exact doubles of Danny and Melinda appeared from thin air. Their doppelgängers wore the same kind of pajamas that they had on.

"Cool!" Danny said.

"Can we touch them?" Melinda said

"Sure, " Doreen said.

Danny and Melinda touched the warm skin and soft hair of their doppelgängers. They thought it was very weird to stare at someone who looked just like they did.

"Can they talk?" Melinda said.

"Not now. I need to do a bit more work on them," Doreen said.

"We must go. We must begin the journey," Brendan said. "Get on your clothes. Pack some jackets and sweaters in a backpack and meet us in the basement in fifteen minutes. We'll make sure that no one sees or stops you."

Danny and Melinda packed as their doubles stood and stared at them silently. They left their doppelgängers in the room, hoping that Doreen would make some improvements and adjustments in them as she promised.

Then they met Brendan and Liam in the hotel's basement.

"Good luck, Miss Boyle and Mr. Boyle. You are very brave," Liam said.

"Let's go, " Brendan said as he led Danny and Melinda out through a service door, down an alley and into the dark Dublin night.

Chapter 9

After leaving the hotel, Brendan used his ghostly powers to transport Danny and Melinda to the ruins of the monastic city of Glendalough south of Dublin. When they arrived, it was pitch black and a light rain was falling. They were in the forest overlooking the ruins.

"Where are we?" Danny asked.

"In Glendalough," Brendan said.

"In Irish, that means 'glen of the two lakes,'" Melinda said.

"Yes, lass, indeed it does," Brendan said. "This is where I must leave you. I can only use my powers to get you here. You must do the rest."

"What are we supposed to do?" Danny said.

"You see that tall stone tower down there? Well, lad, legend has it that inside the tower is a piece of cloth from a robe worn by St. Patrick itself. We need that sacred cloth to help overcome the power of the Celtic chalice."

"How do we get it?" Melinda said.

"That's up to the two of you. I have to go now. If you find the robe, climb the hill near the lake and call my name. Goodbye," Brendan said as he faded from sight, leaving Danny and Melinda alone in the dark woods.

"Well, let's start walking," Danny said. "And put on your rain coat. We can't be getting sick."

Danny pulled his Rivertown Roughnecks baseball cap down tight on his forehead and zipped up his jacket. A wind began to blow, which sprayed raindrops onto his glasses. He pulled out a small flashlight that he always carried with him in his backpack.

Danny and Melinda reached the graveyard and the ruins of the church that stood in front of the stone tower, which was over sixty feet high.

"I don't like this at all," Melinda said. "Maybe we just should have gone home with Mom and Dad."

"It's too late for that," Danny said, thinking about his friend Chip at baseball camp. Chip will never have an adventure like this one to tell me about, Danny thought.

As they crept closer to the wooden door at the base of the tower, they heard branches snapping. They stopped. Their hearts pounded like kettle drums, hard and loud against their chests.

"It's probably just a cat," Danny said. "Let's keep going."

The tower door was locked. So Danny started banging on it with a rock.

"Somebody will hear us," Melinda warned.

"I think I just about got it," Danny said. He had broken the lock. The heavy wooden door swung open. Danny pointed his flashlight through the opening. They saw a small vestibule and a winding stone staircase leading to the top of the tower.

"Where do you think St. Patrick's sacred cloth is, Danny?" Melinda asked.

"I don't know. But I would place it as high up in the tower as possible to protect it, wouldn't you?"

"I think that I would bury it. People would expect it to be at the top of the tower," Melinda said.

"Let's see what's at the top first," Danny said. He was annoyed that Melinda was always contradicting him.

They started climbing the narrow winding stairs higher and higher into the tower. The stone walls and stairs were damp and covered with moss, making the climbing treacherous.

At the very top of the tower was a round chamber. It was completely empty. There were small slits in the thick stone walls.

"Let's go back down. There's nothing here," Melinda said.

They returned to the small vestibule on the ground floor. Danny passed his flashlight over the floor. They saw nothing.

Then they got down on their hands and knees to see if any of the stone were loose. All of the stones were solidly in place.

"Look," Melinda said. She noticed that a small shamrock had been carved into one of the stones. At the end of the stem was an arrow that pointed out the door.

"Maybe the piece of cloth isn't here at all," Melinda said.

"But Brendan said it was," Danny said.

"He said that the legend said it was in the tower. But maybe the legend is wrong. Let's see where the stem of the shamrock is pointing," Melinda said.

So they left the tower and started walking back through the graveyard. Danny pointed his flashlight at each headstone.

"There," Danny said. "Another small shamrock on that stone. The stem is pointing back toward the forest."

They walked on the muddy path back to the forest. On a tree they found a shamrock carved into the bark with its stem pointing down to the ground.

"Let's start digging," Danny said. He and Melinda began clawing at the wet leaves and digging a hole in the mud with their bare hands. The wind was now howling and it was getting colder. Their hands and fingers began to freeze.

About two feet down, they found an old wooden box. They opened it slowly. Inside was a plain brown piece of cloth.

"Do you think this could be it?" Melinda said.

"What else could it be? Those small shamrocks were leading us to something important. Let's take it and climb to the top of the hill and alert Brendan," Danny said, as he placed the cloth in his backpack for safekeeping.

The pouring rain began to seep through their jackets as they trudged up one of the steepest slopes in the Wicklow Mountains. They were damp and they felt miserable.

"Brendan!" they yelled. But Brendan did not appear. They called two more times. Nothing. Finally, on the fourth attempt, Brendan appeared out of the gloom.

"Did you find it?" Brendan asked with great anticipation.

"Yes, but the sacred cloth of St. Patrick wasn't in the tower at all. It was buried beneath a tree in the forest," Melinda said.

"We did a lot of looking around in that creepy old tower for nothing."

"Fancy that, lass," Brendan said. "I guess you can't always trust legends. I'll have a strong word or two with Rory Behan. He's the legend keeper of the ghost world. Old Rory can get confused sometimes. But wasn't that a great adventure anyway?" Brendan said.

"Easy for you to say. You weren't the one getting wet and muddy," Danny said, as he clutched his backpack where he had stored the sacred cloth.

"You are to be congratulated on your first success," said Brendan. "But there are many more journeys you must take."

"Can't we rest for a while?" Melinda said. "I think we deserve it." Melinda's red hair drooped down her forehead and the back of her neck in wet clumps like seaweed. She didn't like being dirty and untidy, but now she was both.

"Indeed you do, lass," Brendan said. "I will take you to Doreen's cottage for some food and a brief nap."

"And a bath," Melinda said.

"And a bath, lass. Oh yes, indeed. I see that the two of you are a bit of a mess. Just grab my hands and I'll take you to Doreen's cottage, which is nice and dry," Brendan said, holding out his spectral hands.

With one touch, Danny and Melinda disappeared from the top of the mountain and into the rainy sky that was as black as ink.

Chapter 10

In the ghost world, news of Danny and Melinda's success in finding the sacred cloth of St. Patrick spread fast. Owen Kildare heard about what they did while spying on the good ghosts in the fields near Lisdoonvarna. "These foolish spirits don't know how to keep a secret," he thought. He quickly reported back to Dermot the Daring.

Dermot was furious when he heard Owen's report. The one thing that a cruel and ambitious ghost like Dermot fears most is combating brave and innocent breathers like Danny and Melinda. He told Owen what he must do.

"We have to call out the spectres," Dermot said. "Only the spectres are evil enough and have the authority to dispose of the children once and for all. If we were to injure or kill the children, we would be sealing our fate. We would be banned to the Forest of Kenmare just as quickly as if the Celtic chalice were destroyed. So we have to get to the little ones before they get to the chalice."

The mere mention of the spectres even made Owen fearful. As a dark ghost, he could scare people and, with the power of the chalice, enter people's bodies to cause mischief. But he could no longer kill breathers. He found it distasteful. He had not intended to kill the two people in the bank robbery. It was an unfortunate accident, he told himself.

Spectres, however, loved to kill. They killed because they died horrible deaths while they were alive, and they wanted revenge. Some died in battles and had their heads or arms chopped off by swords. Others died while setting fires or being executed for murders. If you saw a spectre, you would see how it looked at the moment it died. You would see its pain and hear its agony. All evil people had the potential of becoming spectres when they died. It was just the luck of the draw. Some spirits became spectres. Others— like Dermot and Owen—became members of the dark clan of ghosts. Indeed, they were evil. But not as evil as the bloodthirsty spectres.

Spectres inhabited sea caves and were ordered to stay away from all things—ghostly and human. The spectres' lairs were guarded by an elite band of Dermot's dark council. Dermot knew, however, that the spectres liked to bargain. For if a spectre were released and instructed to kill a breather, their spectral agony would be relieved for one thousand years if they succeeded in their mission. Even though one thousand years was just a blink of an eye in terms of eternity, it was a large enough incentive for the spectres. They longed for any moment free of pain and suffering.

Dermot chose three of the most terrifying spectres to track down Danny and Melinda. Owen could not bear to look at them as they floated out of the sea cave to begin their murderous hunt.

Chapter 11

Danny and Melinda washed and changed their clothes at Doreen's cottage. A large warm fire glowed in her fireplace. Melinda played with Doreen's cat Merlin.

"So how did you become a witch?" Melinda asked as she chewed on a piece of freshly baked bread and stroked Merlin's stomach.

"I was always interested in things that you cannot see. Things that they don't teach you in school," Doreen said. "My Aunt Mary was considered crazy and weird. But that's what really unique people are often called by those who don't understand them. Well, Mary showed me her books about making potions and casting spells."

"Was she a toothless hag?" Danny asked.

"No, she was a lovely beautiful old woman," Doreen said. She pointed to a picture of a woman with soft features, gray hair and a broad smile who wore a red shawl. "That's my Aunt Mary there."

"She's pretty. Like my grandmother," Melinda said. "She doesn't look like she could harm anyone."

"She never did," Doreen said.

"But witches are supposed to be mean and ugly," Danny said. "And they do nasty things like kill cats and turn children into scary beasts, and stuff like that."

"I suppose there are a few witches who use their knowledge and magical powers to do evil things. Just like there are ghosts like Dermot who want to cause trouble," Doreen said. "But most witches and ghosts use their powers for good things. As for myself, I just like to learn about things beyond this world. Are you scared of me?"

"No," Danny said.

"No," Melinda echoed.

"Well, then, there you have it. You're sitting in a witch's house, eating her food and playing with her cat. And you're still alive," Doreen said, smiling.

"She's right, Melinda," Danny said. "I guess you can't believe everything you read."

"Doreen, I've been thinking about something since we first met the ghosts at the hotel. I thought that when you died you went to heaven," Melinda said.

"Or hell," Danny chimed in.

"Oh, now that you've had some food and a warm bath, you're getting all serious on me," Doreen said.

"It's just that you read stories about ghosts and spirits and things like that, but you never in a million years expect to meet one," Melinda said. "It's not what I expected."

"Heaven and hell can mean different things," Doreen said. "Maybe for ghosts like Liam and his friends, heaven is getting a chance to dance for eternity in the hotel's ballroom. To be in a place with other spirits with whom they can share a laugh or two. And for Brendan, heaven is spending most of his time at his favorite golf links. But maybe for Dermot, it's just the opposite. He created his own version of hell because he's so consumed by revenge that he can never really enjoy the spirit state he's been in for the last one thousand years. It must be awful to be angry and hurt for all of that time."

"So heaven or hell might mean different things and be different places for different people," Melinda said.

"That's a very good way of putting it, lass, " Doreen said, gently stroking Melinda's hair with her hand.

"I've been told that I do have a way with words," Melinda said.

Danny rolled his eyes. "For me, heaven would mean having box seats at every Rivertown Roughnecks baseball game for eternity."

Now it was Melinda's turn to roll her eyes in mocking disbelief.

"How about you, Melinda?" Doreen asked.

"Unlike Danny, I haven't thought that far ahead. I don't know what to say. Maybe I don't know yet," Melinda said.

"Neither do I lass. Neither do I," Doreen said.

"When will Brendan be back?" Danny asked.

"First thing in the morning. He wants to play a round of golf before the sun comes up," Doreen said. "So you two better get some rest."

"Where will we be going next?" Danny asked.

"I cannot tell you that," Doreen said. "You'll find out soon enough. I think it's better that way."

Doreen showed Danny and Melinda to their beds. Before they fell asleep, they thought of Rivertown. They wondered if their doppelgängers were behaving, and if their parents had noticed anything different about them. They didn't want to return home and be punished for something that they hadn't done.

Alone in her livingroom in her favorite rocking chair in front of the fire, Doreen began to doze off herself. But she awoke suddenly when she felt a sharp chill drill into her skin. She sensed that something was wrong. She walked to her front door, open it and peered across the dark fields. She saw nothing. But the three spectres that Dermot had sent saw her.

Chapter 12

Just before dawn, Doreen awakened Danny and Melinda. Brendan had arrived to escort them to the site of their next task.

Rubbing the sleep from her eyes, Melinda asked Brendan where they would be going.

"I'll be taking ya to the far north of Ireland, lass," Brendan said. "We'll be going to County Donegal, where the winds howl off the ocean something fierce. There in a cave high on a cliff above the boiling Atlantic Ocean lives a giant called McGinty. The ring that he wears has the power we need to fight the golden chalice. You have to get the ring from McGinty."

"How big a giant is he?" Danny asked.

"Twice as tall as any human being and three times as mean," Brendan said. "Legend has it that he catches huge fish from the sea with his bare hands and eats them in two or three large bites—bones and all."

"Stop it, Brendan," Doreen said. "You'll be scaring the children now."

"I'm just telling them the truth," Brendan responded. "They have to know what they're up against. They have to think of a plan to get McGinty's ring. That is, unless they're scared and want to quit now."

"We're not scared, are we Danny?" Melinda said. "We weren't scared at the tower in Glendalough, and we won't be scared of some giant."

"No, we're not scared," Danny said.

"Well, you've got plenty of pluck. I'll give you that," Brendan said. "Here, touch my finger. It's time to go."

"Goodbye," Doreen said.

Danny and Melinda hugged Doreen, who had been so kind to them. They walked over to Brendan and touched his finger. They vanished from Doreen's cottage. Then suddenly they were on a wind-swept cliff in Donegal. The green Atlantic Ocean pounded the rocky shore hundreds of feet below them.

"Where's McGinty's cave?" Danny asked.

"It's down there," Brendan said, pointing to a steep, rocky path they led from the top of the cliff to an opening one hundred feet below them. "I have to leave you know. Give me a yell when you have got the ring. Good luck!" Then he was gone.

Danny and Melinda zipped up their jackets and pulled their hoods over their heads to protect themselves from the brisk wind.

"How are we going to get the ring off a finger of a giant?" Melinda asked.

"Let's think a minute before we hike down there," Danny said. "We can't fight him. He's too big and too mean, at least that's what Brendan says."

"Maybe Brendan's wrong. He didn't have all of the facts straight about where St. Patrick's sacred cloth was hidden," Melinda said.

"That's true. But people aren't called giants for nothing. McGinty must be really big."

"But maybe he's not mean," Melinda insisted.

"Let's just say that he is. How do we get the ring from him?"

"We can steal it while he's asleep," Melinda said.

"That's a good idea. Or we can trade something for it. Maybe McGinty doesn't even know that the ring has any special powers," Danny said.

"Yeah, maybe he doesn't," Melinda said. She was actually impressed by the way Danny was thinking, but she would never tell him this. She liked to keep her big brother off balance and guessing about what she would do or say next.

"If we had to, what could we trade McGinty for the ring?" Danny thought out loud. Danny opened his backpack. He had some clothes, a flashlight and some guide books and maps. Nothing that a giant would like, he thought. "I think we're out of luck when it comes to trading."

"Then I guess we'll just have to take the ring without him knowing it," Melinda said. "Let's go. It's cold up here. Some summer weather."

They descended carefully down the steep path. The wind that whipped the cliff nearly blew Danny and Melinda into the ocean several times. They gasped with fear. They thought that they would slip to their deaths with each step. So they held each other's hand to feel more secure. Finally, they arrived at the entrance to McGinty's cave. They were cold and wet. Their legs and arms ached because they were so tense with fear.

"I can't see anything," Melinda said.

"I don't want to use the flashlight. McGinty might see us," Danny said.

"But we might trip over something and hurt ourselves or make a noise that the giant hears," Melinda said. "Let's just take the chance of using the flashlight."

"OK," Danny agreed. "But we have to be very quiet."

With the flashlight turned on, Danny and Melinda crept through a high, wide passage. Scattered on the floor were huge fish bones. The cave had the smell of rotting fish.

The passage gradually widened into a cavern. There was a large pile of straw and an old blanket rolled up in the corner. But there was no sign of McGinty.

"This is where he must sleep," Melinda said. "Where do you think he is?"

"It's early in the morning. He's probably out fishing," Danny said. "Let's hide behind that pile of rocks and wait."

They waited one hour. And then another. There was no sign of McGinty. Then, after three hours had passed, they heard a sound of something being dragged. McGinty appeared carrying a torch in one hand and dragging a large fish by the tail fin in the other hand. He was at least twelve feet high. He had wild black hair and eyes and a huge wart on his nose. His clothes were old and ripped. His large feet were bare. There on the last finger of his right hand was a giant blue ring.

He placed his torch in a holder in the rock and sat down on the straw bed. From their hiding place, Danny and Melinda then saw McGinty eat the large fish in two gigantic bites—bones and all—just like Brendan said he would do. After eating the fish, McGinty belched loudly and lay down on the straw, wrapping himself in the blanket. He soon fell asleep and began to snore. The sound of his snoring echoed in the cavern.

"Now is our chance to get the ring," Melinda whispered. "Go ahead."

"Why me?" Danny said. "Why don't you do it?"

"Because you're stronger than me. And I can be on the lookout for another giant. Maybe there's another one. You never know," Melinda said.

"Fine. But I just think you're scared. Stay here," Danny said, giving her the flashlight.

Danny crawled slowly across the stone floor to McGinty's foul-smelling bed of straw. He tugged at the large blue ring, but it wouldn't come off of McGinty's finger. He was afraid that if he pulled too hard he would awaken the snoring giant. He braced his feet and gave the ring one final pull. He fell backward. The ring flew over his head and smacked against the rock. He quickly grabbed it and ran back to the place where Melinda was hiding.

"I've got it. Let's go," Danny said, breathing heavily.

As they were about to leave the cave, McGinty awoke. He stretched and groaned. Then he noticed that his precious ring was missing. He jumped up quickly and cried out: "My ring. My beautiful ring." He started searching in the straw. Then he stopped and started sniffing the air.

"I know that someone is here!" McGinty bellowed. "Whoever you are, I know that you stole my ring. I'll kill you!"

"Let's make a run for it!" Danny pleaded with Melinda.

"No, wait. I have an idea," Melinda said, as she grabbed the ring and stood up.

"Melinda, are you nuts?" Danny said.

"Mr. McGinty, over here," Melinda said. "We've got your ring. But we're not going to steal it. We just want to borrow it."

"Who dares enter my home and take my ring?" McGinty said, bending down and staring straight at Melinda with his enormous coal-black eyes.

"I'm Melinda Boyle and this is my brother Danny," Melinda said. "We just want to borrow your ring. It has some magic powers that will help us defeat this evil ghost named Dermot. The good ghosts of Ireland sent us here."

"I will kill you!" McGinty roared again. "No one comes to my cave."

"You must get lonely then," Melinda said. "It's cold here and so far away from other houses. Don't you get lonely?"

McGinty was so surprised that this little girl was talking to him and that she wasn't afraid of him that he didn't know what to say.

He backed away from Melinda and responded in a quieter voice: "Sometimes I would like to have visitors. But other people always laugh and stare at me. No one bothers me here."

"We're not making fun of you, are we Danny?" Melinda said.

"No, Mr. McGinty," Danny said.

"I have an idea. We can tell our ghost friends to come and visit you from time to time to keep you company. They don't care that you're a giant. They might try to scare you now and then. After all, they are ghosts and that's what ghosts like to do. But overall, they're really quite pleasant," Melinda said. "You're not afraid of ghosts, are you?"

"No!" McGinty said. "Not me!"

"Good. Then it's all settled," Melinda said. "We'll keep your beautiful ring until our mission is over. And then we'll make sure that it is returned to you safe and sound. It obviously means a lot to you."

"My grandfather gave the ring to my father, who gave it to me many years ago. I like the color. Like the sky and the ocean. He told me that one day it would bring me good luck. I long for that day," McGinty said.

"Maybe today is that day. I mean meeting Melinda and me. We can introduce you to people—I mean ghosts—who won't make fun of you. You can trust us to keep the ring safe," Danny said, placing the ring in his backpack with the sacred cloth.

"We have to go now," Melinda said.

"Are you sure that I will be getting visitors? The ghosts," McGinty said.

"We'll make sure of it," Melinda said. "Goodbye."

"Goodbye," McGinty said, waving his giant hand.

Danny and Melinda climbed back up the path to the top of the cliff.

"I can't believe what just happened," Danny said. "How did you know he wouldn't eat us like he did that fish?"

"I didn't," Melinda said. "But I sensed that he wasn't all that mean. Intuition I guess."

"Yeah, right. Sure. More like dumb luck," Danny said skeptically. "Let's call Brendan and get out of here before McGinty changes his mind."

Before they could call for Brendan, however, they were surrounded by the three spectres that had been hunting them.

Chapter 13

Unlike Brendan, Liam and the other ghosts that Danny and Melinda had seen, the spectres were hideous in their appearance. One had its left limb severed. Another had a huge gaping wound in its chest. And the third looked as if its spectral body had been burned from head to foot. A cold swirling wind, like a tornado, whipped around them and Danny and Melinda.

Danny and Melinda both screamed with fright when the spectres appeared. They tried to run, but they were stopped by the icy, evil presence of the spectres.

The spectre with the wound in its chest spoke in a high-pitched howl, like that of a wolf that had been caught in a trap. It made Danny and Melinda's skin crawl and hearts skip a beat.

"Give us the cloth and the ring," it said slowly.

Danny and Melinda said nothing.

"Give us the cloth and the ring," the spectre repeated, grabbing for Danny's backpack.

Danny began to run across the empty fields. Melinda followed, but she couldn't keep up. Danny kept running without looking back until he heard Melinda scream. He turned around quickly and saw that two of the spectres had grabbed Melinda and were carrying her into the sky.

"Put her down!" Danny yelled.

A frigid laugh came from the spectres. They carried Melinda high over the cliff, which dropped several hundred feet to the ocean below. They dangled her in the air by her arms. Melinda was too scared even to scream.

"Give us the ring and the cloth and we will let her live," one of the spectres said.

Danny wasn't sure if he could believe the spectre. He didn't want Melinda to get hurt, but he promised the good ghosts that he would gather what they needed to defeat Dermot the Daring.

Danny decided that he had to save Melinda, so he opened his backpack, placed McGinty's ring and St. Patrick's cloth on the moist ground and told the leader of the spectres to come and take them. But first they must lower Melinda to the ground.

As the lead spectre approached Danny, the other two spectres suddenly dropped Melinda. Danny's heart sank as he saw Melinda fall out of sight over the edge of the cliff. Her screams grew fainter as the sarcastic laughs of the spectres grew louder.

Angrily, Danny threw the sacred cloth of St. Patrick at the lead spectre as it drew near. The cloth hit the spectre, which burst into flames. The air boomed with the spectre's agonized screams. The flames grew white hot. Then the lead spectre was gone. Seeing what had happened, the remaining spectres rose into the sky and disappeared.

Danny rushed to the edge of the cliff. Tears flowed down his face. He yelled: "No! "No!"

He peered over the side. To his amazement, Melinda was safe. She was being carried up the steep rocky path by McGinty, who cradled her in his giant arms.

"Melinda, you're OK," Danny said as he rushed to embrace his sister.

"Get off of me!" Melinda cried. "None of that mushy stuff. Our friend here snatched me out of the air as I was falling. Not even a scratch."

"Thank you," Danny said.

"It was nothing. I heard a ruckus. And when I poked my head out of the cave, I saw the little lass here falling. So I stuck my arms out and she fell right in— light as a feather," McGinty said. "Now what were those things that were after you?"

"I don't know," Danny said. "But I destroyed one of them

when I threw St. Patrick's cloth at it. Then the other disappeared."

"We better call for Brendan and get out of here," Melinda said. She then turned to McGinty: "Just so you know, Brendan is one of out ghosts friends."

"Is he now," McGinty said. "Well, where is he?"

"Watch this," Danny said. "Brendan! "Brendan!"

Brendan appeared. "Do you have the blue ring?"

"Yes, of course we do," Melinda said. "Mr. McGinty here was kind enough to lend it to us."

"That's mighty kind of ya, sir," Brendan said.

"We promised to return it as soon as possible. We also promised that you and some of your friends would come and visit Mr. McGinty from time to time. He gets awfully lonely here, " Danny explained.

"We'd be glad to. If you don't mind an unexpected fright or two. We are ghosts after all," said Brendan.

"Not at all," McGinty said.

"Grand," Brendan said. "Now let's go."

"Just one more thing," Melinda said as she walked toward Brendan with her hands on her hips. She looked displeased. "Some really ugly ghosts tried to kill me. And I'm sure that they wanted to steal the cloth and the ring. What do you know about that?"

Then Danny and Melinda described their encounter with the spectres.

"This is bad," Brendan said, scratching his head after listening to their story about the spectres. "Dermot knows what we're up to. We have to be extra careful from here on. I'll have to talk with Doreen to see what she recommends. Now, children, let's be off!"

Chapter 14

Brendan deposited Danny and Melinda back at Doreen's in the mid-afternoon. Although the sun sets very late during an Irish summer, the day was dark and rainy. Clouds hung low like dirty sheets over the green pastures near Lisdoonvarna.

Danny and Melinda were wet, cold and tired when they arrived back at Doreen's cottage. They changed clothes. When they came back into the livingroom, Doreen had hot chocolate and cake ready for them. As usual, a comforting fire was crackling in the fireplace. Merlin the cat rubbed himself against Danny and Melinda's legs as if to say: "Hello and welcome back." Then he went and stretched out on his favorite spot on the rug in front of the fire.

Danny and Melinda told Doreen about what had happened at McGinty's cave and how the spectres were out to kill them and stop them on their mission. Doreen could see both the fatigue and fear in their faces. She thought that they were brave little souls.

"Would you like to hear a story?" Doreen said. Doreen loved to tell tales to children, just like her Aunt Mary used to love to recite stories to her. A good story could take your mind off of your troubles, Doreen always had thought.

Danny and Melinda nodded "yes" with enthusiasm. They sat next to each other on the sofa, under a blanket with their steaming hot chocolate on the table in front of them.

"In the small town of Macroom, there once lived an old man named Sean Hanratty. But everyone called him 'The Rat.' He had a long, narrow face and small black eyes. He moved from place to place very quickly and quietly. 'Just like a rat crawling along a wall,' people used to joke," Doreen said.

"No one knew how Hanratty made a living or how his father or grandfather before him made a living. They just knew that every few months a truck would pull up to the large barn on his property, and then it would drive away. When someone had the courage to ask Hanratty what he did, he replied: 'I keep to myself.' He then tipped his cap and walked away. He never bothered anyone. But the villagers of Macroom thought that he must be keeping dark secrets hidden in that barn."

"A few men who had too much to drink would sneak up to the barn to get a glimpse of what was inside, but the barn had no windows and the door was always locked. And Hanratty had a border collie called Cyril who prowled the property. Over the years, he took a bite out of the backsides of quite a few young men in Macroom."

"As time went on, people stopped paying much attention to Hanratty. And that was just the way Hanratty liked it," Doreen continued. She could see that Danny and Melinda were struggling to stay awake. Her house was warm, quiet and cozy—a perfect place to catch a few winks.

"It just so happened that a boy named Simon Connell lived on the property next to Hanratty's. Simon was thirteen years old. His mother and father had told him awful stories about 'The Rat.' They told him that Hanratty must have been hiding dead bodies in his barn. Or that he was involved in some kind of black magic. Simon was afraid of Hanratty. He kept his distance from him through the years."

"But Simon also didn't get along very well with his father. You see, Simon loved to paint, and he was very good at it. In his small room in the back of the Connells' house, Simon would create glorious paintings of the Irish landscape and scenes from Irish folklore. But Simon's father hated to see Simon wasting his time with paintings. His father wanted Simon to take over the farm and raise sheep. But Simon never really liked farm life. He dreamed of something different," Doreen said.

"Simon and his father got into terrible fights that made

Simon's mother and younger brother and sister cry. On the darkest winter day, Simon couldn't take his father's lectures anymore, so he ran out of the house and into the fields. He jumped right over the stone fence that enclosed the fields and started running along a small stream that flowed through Sean Hanratty's property. Simon was running fast, but he wasn't sure where he was going. It was pitch black. He didn't see the slippery stones in front of him. He tripped and fell into the cold stream, hitting his head on the rocks. The next thing Simon knew he was inside Hanratty's barn," Doreen said. Then she stopped. Danny and Melinda were trying to stay awake, but their heads were slumping on their chests.

"Don't stop," Melinda said as she rubbed her eyes and sat up straight.

"What happened to Simon?" Danny said.

"The tale can wait," Doreen said. "You must rest. Come on, move along."

"But it's still daytime," Melinda protested.

"It's time for you to get some rest," Doreen said. "I won't be hearing nothing more from you. Don't give me no trouble now."

After Danny and Melinda went to sleep, Brendan paid Doreen a visit. They discussed very important matters of spirits and magic.

Chapter 15

Brendan arrived at dawn the next morning to escort Danny and Melinda to another location—the Beara Peninsula in the southwest part of Ireland.

"This time your task is to retrieve a shawl from a mermaid," Brendan said. "A mermaid's shawl has great powers that we need against Dermot and the Celtic chalice. You do know what a mermaid is?"

"Yes," Danny said. "It's a woman who is half fish and half person."

"That's correct. Excellent," Brendan said. "Now mermaids like to sit on remote, sunny beaches and sing songs while relaxing in the sun. Just remember one important thing: never believe what a mermaid tells you. They are legendary tricksters."

"Before you go, I have something very important to give you," Doreen said. She handed Danny a small mirror.

"What are we supposed to do with this?" Danny said.

"I've cast spell on this mirror. If I did it correctly, it will help you fight against the spectres, should they return," Doreen said.

"And they will. You can count on that," Brendan said.

"If the spectres attack you, point this mirror at them. They will not see their reflection as they are now, but as they were when they were alive. They will see themselves before they were maimed. The sight and memory of a time when they were whole human beings should drive them mad. And drive them away from you forever. At least that's what my book of spells told me," Doreen said.

"I hope your spell works. I don't want to be dangled over a cliff again," Melinda said.

"Come now," Brendan said. "It's time to go mermaid hunting."

In a split second, Danny and Melinda found themselves in a desolate bog, which is a wet piece of ground that feels like a sponge. In the distance, they could hear the ocean pounding against the rocks. Luckily for them, it was a rare bright and sunny Irish summer day.

Danny and Melinda began walking across the bog to the ocean. Their shoes made squishy sounds as they went.

Halfway across the bog, they felt the earth quiver beneath their feet. Then before they could react, a giant shaggy-haired, foul-smelling horse rose up out of the bog and started charging Danny and Melinda.

"It's a pooka," Danny said. "Run!" Pookas live in bogs, which they consider their territory. They don't like trespassers. And they get very angry when some unfortunate person wanders into a bog that they claim as their private realm.

Danny and Melinda ran as fast as they could through the bog, but it seemed that the harder they tried the deeper their shoes sunk into the wet, mushy ground. The pooka gained on them. He came right up behind Danny, grabbed his pants in his snarling teeth and lifted him up off the ground. Then the pooka began twirling around in circles — faster and faster.

Danny begged Melinda to keep running. She made it to the other side of the bog. She stood there as the pooka continued to spin like a top. Then the pooka let Danny go. Danny went flying across the bog like an arrow shot from a bow. He flew over Melinda's head, landing in a heap behind her. In the distance, the pooka let out a high-pitched whinny — as if it were laughing — pounded the ground with its hoofs and then disappeared beneath the bog.

Melinda ran to Danny. "Are you all right?" Melinda asked.

"My head hurts," Danny said. "And I feel really dizzy."

Melinda noticed a large bump on Danny's forehead that was swelling to the size of a golf ball. But otherwise he seemed fine.

"You'll live," Melinda said. "Let's keep going."

"Thanks for the concern," Danny said.

As Danny and Melinda neared the rocky shore of the Beara Peninsula, they stopped talking and crept behind large boulders. They didn't see anything except for some small fishing boats in the distance. The air was filled with the sound of the waves crashing on the shore.

"Did you hear that?" Melinda said.

"What?" Danny replied.

"Are you deaf?" Melinda said. "Someone is singing. Over there. Let's go."

Walking about fifty feet to their right, Danny and Melinda suddenly stopped. There on a large rock sat a mermaid, singing a haunting Irish melody. She had a long green tail with scales. But from the waist up, she was a beautiful woman with long brown hair and giant blue eyes that sparkled in the summer sun. Next to her on the rock was her golden shawl.

"How are we going to get the shawl?" Melinda said.

Danny lowered his head a moment and thought of a plan. "You go out and talk to her. You know, distract her. Keep her occupied. I'll get the shawl then," Danny said.

"Sounds like a good plan," Melinda said. "Can you really be my brother?"

"Just go," Danny said. With his head throbbing, he wasn't in the mood to deal with Melinda's sarcastic remarks.

Melinda walked toward the mermaid. "That's a pretty song," Melinda said to the mermaid. "What's it about?"

"And who might you be, lass?" the mermaid said.

"I'm Melinda. I'm here on vacation from America," Melinda said.

"Well, Melinda from America, the song is about a handsome prince's love for a beautiful peasant girl who doesn't love him."

"Sounds sad."

"Those are the best kind of songs."

"I prefer happy songs."

"I don't know many of those. I'm Irish after all."

"Can you jump in the air like a dolphin? I like the way

dolphins leap out of the water and make a huge splash. Can you do that?" Melinda said.

"Why would I want to, lass? I'm enjoying myself here on this sunny rock."

"So I guess you can't do it," Melinda said.

"Of course I can," the mermaid replied, offended that Melinda didn't believe she could swim as well as a dolphin. "If I leap out of the water for you, will you be on your way and leave me in peace?"

"OK. It's a deal," Melinda said.

The mermaid crawled down from the rock and disappeared under the sea, leaving her shawl behind her.

"Danny, come on. Get the shawl," Melinda said.

Danny rushed out from his hiding place and snatched the beautiful golden shawl. He stuffed it into his backpack.

"Let's go!" Danny said.

In the sea, the mermaid rocketed out of the ocean, performed a graceful somersault and then dove back into the waves in a great splash. She surfaced and yelled to Melinda: "Now wasn't that a grand show, lass? A dolphin couldn't have done it better."

Melinda yelled back: "That was wonderful. Thank you. But just so you don't become concerned, we've borrowed your pretty shawl. We need it for something important. We'll return it as soon as we can."

"My shawl. My beautiful golden shawl. Please give it back to me. I will teach you how to sing as lovely as I do," the mermaid pleaded.

"Don't listen to her, Melinda. Let's just keep going," Danny said.

"And I'll teach you how to swim even better than a dolphin," the mermaid said as she began to cry and moan in despair.

"She's crying, Danny. Maybe there's something else that has the same power as her shawl. We could use that instead. We should give the shawl back to her. She looks so sad," Melinda said.

"No. You know what Brendan said. It's just a trick. Keep going," Danny said.

Melinda kept turning around and looking at the mermaid sobbing and rolling around in agony on the shore. When they reached the edge of the bog, Danny yelled for Brendan to appear.

"We've got the golden shawl," Danny said after Brendan materialized over the bog.

"Excellent job once again," Brendan said. "What happened to your head?"

"We had a run in with the pooka that lives here. I've read that they could be nasty. This time everything I had read was true, " Danny said.

"Pookas are bloody awful beasts. That's a fact," Brendan said. Then he looked at Melinda. "Why so sad, lass?"

"The mermaid really loved her golden shawl. We shouldn't have taken it," Melinda said.

"But we need it more than she does at the moment," Brendan said. "We will return it to her safe and sound. Now don't you worry."

"Promise?"

"I promise, " Brendan said. "Any spectres in sight?"

"Not one," Danny replied.

"Good. But you can be sure they're plotting something. Keep on guard. Now Doreen said that she has a story she wants to finish telling you. Let's go."

Chapter 16

"Simon awoke lying on an old sofa in Hanratty's barn," Doreen said, continuing the story of young Simon Connell and the mysterious Sean Hanratty. Danny and Melinda sat quietly, paying close attention to Doreen's tale.

"Sitting next to him was Hanratty's dog Cyril, who barked when Simon started to arise. 'Where am I?' Simon asked. His head began pounding as he tried to stand. 'You're in my studio, young fella,' said Hanratty. 'Can I get you a cup of tea? You had quite a fall. Good thing ol' Cyril and I were out for a walk.'"

"'What are you going to do to me?' Simon asked. He stared at Hanratty, who stood there exhibiting his rat-like nose and big barrel chest with grey hairs sprouting out of it like weeds. Hanratty's boots were old and muddy."

"'I'll be doing nothing except making sure that you're fine. Then I'll walk on over to your house and tell your parents what happened,' Hanratty said."

"'No, please don't. I was running away,' Simon said."

"'That's what I thought. I can hear the yelling and the carrying on over there,' Hanratty said. 'But your Da and Ma are probably worried. So you better get home if you can walk. Work things out when you get there. Can't have you stay here. No, that wouldn't do. Wouldn't do at all.'"

"'No, my Da doesn't like my painting. He wants me to raise sheep like him,' Simon explained. 'And I don't want to.'"

"'Nothing wrong with that, if you're so inclined,' Hanratty said."

"'I'm not inclined,' Simon said."

"'Neither was I, young fella, when I was your age.'"

"'What do you do here? People tell all kinds of stories about what goes on at this place.'"

"'I know. But people in a small village like this are so suspicious of someone who does something different. I just chose to keep to myself. Life's simpler that way.'"

"'So what do you do?' Simon asked again."

"'You're not afraid of me. I can see that. You look like the curious sort. So follow me through that door there.'"

"Hanratty led Simon through two large doors into a cavernous art studio that was filled with huge stone and metal sculptures of great and famous people in Irish history and legends. Simon had never seen anything so wonderful. Hanratty was an artist like him. A real artist was living right down the road for all of those years and he never knew," Doreen said. Then she continued with the story.

"'I can't believe it. You made these?' Simon asked."

"'That's what I do. That's my life,' Hanratty explained."

"'So that's why those huge trucks come here—to pick up your artwork. Why don't you want to share your sculptures with the people who live in Macroom?'"

"'It's just easier that way. Maybe people won't like what I do. That would make me sad. I'd rather that they make fun of me than of my work.'"

"'Can you teach me how to do this? I want to learn to be a great artist like you.'"

"'I don't think so. It wouldn't work. Cyril and I have a nice quiet life here,' Hanratty replied, scratching the hairs on his chest and snorting. But then Hanratty saw the empty look in Simon's eyes. He saw himself in that young boy."

"Eventually, Sean Hanratty did take Simon Connell on as an art student. Through the years, Sean's talent grew. And he convinced Hanratty to show the mayor of Macroom his work. The mayor was so impressed that one of Hanratty's sculptures sits in the town square today. And nobody called Hanratty 'The Rat' anymore. They tipped their caps to him and whispered that he's the famous artist who lives down the road," Doreen explained. "Hanratty smiled politely and Cyril wagged his tail."

"What happened to Simon?" Danny asked.

"Simon went on to art school in Dublin. But he did return to Macroom. When Sean Hanratty died, he left his farm and studio to Simon, who lives there today with his wife, son and daughter. Now Sean is the great artist of Macroom," Doreen said.

"So Sean Hanratty wasn't a mean old man after all," Melinda said.

"No he wasn't," Doreen said.

"Sometimes people just surprise you," Danny said.

"That's for sure," Melinda said. "Can we have more hot chocolate?"

Chapter 17

Danny and Melinda spent a delightful summer day relaxing with Doreen. A warm breeze gently caressed the grass in the fields while delicate clouds floated across the sky. Danny sat on the porch and read a few chapters in his book about the history of baseball. Occasionally he looked up to see Melinda, Doreen and the cat Merlin playing in the fields. Merlin would try to catch mice, but he was not having much luck. From across the fields, Danny could hear Melinda's loud cackling laughter. He was glad that she was enjoying herself.

Toward sunset Brendan appeared. This time, however, he did not tell Danny and Melinda about their next journey. He had a different surprise.

"Would you like to see a bit of hurling?" Brendan said.

"What's hurling?" Melinda replied. "And will I like it?"

"I know what hurling is," Danny said. "It's like hockey—only it's played on a grass field—or 'pitch' as they call it here—with a small ball and a wooden stick. The stick is called a hurley. The game is at least two thousand years old. We've got to see it at least once, Melinda. Is there a pitch with lights around here?"

"Not exactly," Brendan said. "We're going to see an all-star hurling match played by ghosts. They don't need lights."

"Cool!" Danny said. Although hurling wasn't baseball, it will do, he thought.

Brendan transported Danny and Melinda to a large pitch that was completely dark except for the shapes of fifteen ghostly players for each team—one dressed in bright blue striped jerseys and the other in green. A large crowd of ghosts had gathered on the sidelines cheering for their favorite team and players. It was a magnificent pageant.

The match had already started. Players were flying up and down the pitch, going right through one another. When you're a ghost, there are no big, bone-crushing collisions like when you're alive. One burly ghost named Seamus had the ball called a "sliothar" balanced on the end of the hurley. He positioned himself for a score. He fired the sliothar under the crossbar, past the diving goalkeeper and into the back of the net. The blue team had three points.

"If they're ghosts, how come they are playing with real bats and balls?" Melinda asked.

"They're not bats. They're called hurleys," Danny corrected her.

"Whatever," Melinda said. "So Brendan, what's up with that?"

"It's simple, lass," Brendan explained. "A real hurley and sliothar are more fun. They give the game its true feel. Holding a real hurley makes the players feel alive, so to speak. We may be dead, but we still like to recall the feel of wood, the touch of silk and the smell of a Christmas goose."

The hurling match featured lots of scoring. In the end, the blue team defeated the green team 24 to 21. Danny loved it. The match made him think about the warm summer nights he spent watching the Rivertown Roughnecks play the Waterville Buffaloes with his friend Chip. Even Melinda cheered with the gathered spirits.

By the end of the match, however, Danny and Melinda were ready to return to Doreen's and go to sleep.

"Well, that was a nice break from what you've been doing, don't you think?" Brendan said, as he waved goodbye to his ghostly friends who were departing the hurling pitch. "There's a crisis and all happening with Dermot, but you still need to have a little fun. All work and no play is bad for the soul. But tomorrow you will have one more job to do. This time, you need to bring back the stone of truth. Anyone who is placed on the stone must tell the truth. Therefore, it's a powerful force against the Celtic chalice, which breeds lies and deception in those who touch it. The stone can be found in a prehistoric burial site near Doolin. It should be a simple enough job for you two. Now let's be off. Doreen's waiting up for you."

Chapter 18

Although Dermot was discouraged that the spectres had not yet killed Danny and Melinda, he was confident that they would ultimately succeed. Since the spectres never failed in their missions, Dermot turned his attentions to greater concerns.

"I am disappointed in certain members of our council," Dermot told his closest confidant Brian Burke. Dermot and Brian were hovering in the darkened office of the Irish prime minister. Light drizzle dripped down the windows.

"What do you mean?" Brian asked.

"I mean that there are certain spirits who don't, how shall I say it, live up to the standards of power and evil that they should," Dermot said. "Some spirits are more timid and weak than I had imagined."

"Like who?" Brian asked.

"One spirit leaps to mind: Owen Kildare. He can be as excitable and enthusiastic as a little puppy, but like a puppy he has no real killer instinct. He just wants affection," Dermot said.

"But Owen Kildare is known as Killer Kildare. He killed two people in cold blood during a bank robbery. That sounds vicious to me," Brian said.

"That's nothing. That's child's play. Look at what we have accomplished. What Kildare has done pales in comparison. To succeed fully in my plan, I must have spirits whose evil knows no bounds, who can ensure that we will in fact remake Ireland in our image. I don't believe that Owen Kildare can help us. We must get rid of him," Dermot said.

"But he's a spirit. He's already dead," Brian said.

"That's true. But he can be banished and neutralized. I know of dark secrets of which no other spirit is aware. There is a place called the jail of Slieve from which no ghost can escape. That's where Owen Kildare will spend eternity," Dermot said.

But Brian Burke was not the only spirit who had heard Dermot's menacing declaration. Owen was hovering silently outside the window. He had heard every oily word that Dermot had spoken. He knew what he must do. Dermot would not betray him. Dermot the Daring had underestimated Owen Kildare.

Chapter 19

The town of Doolin sits near an area called the Burren, a land resembling a barren moonscape where jagged hills that look like crumbling buildings sit above fields exploding with wildflowers. Ancient tribes roamed the Burren and built small villages out of the stone.

Burial sites litter the fields. Most are just curiosities for the tourists. But the ghosts knew that hidden in one gravesite was a stone that can compel someone to tell the truth. Such a stone would be a powerful force against the Celtic chalice that Dermot used to do his evil work.

Brendan took Danny and Melinda to a barren field and pointed them toward a pile of rocks that looked like a small house that leaned to the right.

"The stone of truth is supposed to be there," Brendan said.

"But there are stones everywhere. How will we know which one is the stone of truth?" Danny said.

"If something strange begins to happen, then you'll know you found it," Brendan said.

"But won't there be ghosts? After all, it is a burial place. Won't they be angry?" Danny said.

"I know all of the ghosts in this part of Ireland. The spirits of the folks who are buried here moved out centuries ago. I believe they haunt southern France now. They like socializing with the ghosts of the people who made the pictures of animals on cave walls," Brendan explained. "Good luck." And then he was gone.

"Well, let's go. This is the last thing we have to get. Then we can go home. I miss Mom and Dad, don't you?" Melinda said.

"Yes, I do too," Danny replied.

"And who knows what problems our doppelgängers are causing for us," Melinda added.

Danny and Melinda walked to the burial site and looked around. They saw a pile of stones. So they began picking up stones one by one. Nothing happened. They moved dozens of stones. Their arms began to ache.

"We're getting nowhere, Danny," Melinda said.

"Just keep looking. It has to be here somewhere," Danny said.

After another thirty minutes of moving stones around, Danny found a stone that had a very smooth surface. It was a stone that looked man-made.

"Look!" Danny yelled. "I think this is the one."

"How do you know?" Melinda said.

"Well, Brendan told us that something strange would happen if we found the right one," Danny said. "But I don't see or feel anything. Maybe I'm wrong."

A second after those words came out of Danny's mouth, the stone was pulled from his hands by an invisible force. The stone flew high into the air. Then a horrible laugh rang throughout the Burren. One of the two remaining spectres sent by Dermot to kill Danny and Melinda had snatched the stone of truth.

"The spectres!" Melinda yelled in fear.

The spectres began hurling heavy stones at Danny and Melinda. They ducked and covered their heads with their hands. The stones were smashed to pieces on the rocky ground. A direct hit by one of the stones would kill them.

"We have to run, Danny," Melinda said.

"Where? There's no place to hide here. It's all open space here," Danny said. Then he thought of the mirror that Doreen had given him. He pulled it out of his backpack and pointed it at one of the spectres that was holding the stone of truth.

In the mirror, the spectre saw what it had looked like when it was a young boy—full of youthful energy and happiness. The spectre screamed in agony as if it had been shot. The sight of itself as an innocent child who had not done mean and evil things was so painful that the spectre began to fade away. It stopped screaming and began crying, and then it slowly began to fade away until it had disappeared. The stone of truth fell to the ground.

Danny quickly looked for the other spectre. He was ready to point the mirror at it. The remaining spectre saw what had happened to its evil companion, however, so it bolted in fear. It could not bear seeing itself in a time when it was not evil.

Melinda ran and picked up the stone of truth. "Are they really gone?" she asked.

"It looks that way. Doreen's spell worked great," Danny said.

They called for Brendan.

"You have found it already?" he said. "I barely was able to get through three holes of golf. Let's go back to Doreen's. Tonight, we shall go to the Macgillycuddy Mountains to end Dermot's reign of terror once and for all."

Chapter 20

"The time has finally come," Doreen said. *"You have gathered all of the items whose power can overturn the evil force of Boru's Celtic chalice."*

"Why these things?" Danny asked.

"The cloth of St. Patrick represents the sacred. The ring of the giant McGinty stands for family love and remembrance. The mermaid's golden shawl symbolizes beauty. And the stone of truth, well, you know what that means," Doreen said.

"All of these things together will defeat the black powers that Dermot has been using to turn this country upside down," Brendan said.

"Do we know they will work?" Melinda said.

"My research into magic powers tells me that they will," Doreen said. "But I guess we'll soon find out, lass."

"But how will we know where the chalice is? It's supposed to be hidden, right?" Danny asked.

"In that we've have a little help," Brendan said. "Let me introduce you to Owen Kildare."

"Dia duit," Owen said.

"That means 'Hello,'" Melinda said.

"She's a right smart young lass," Owen said.

"Don't encourage her," Danny, Brendan and Doreen all said together, laughing. Even Melinda smiled at first. Then she frowned and put her hands on her hips, which was her way of saying: "Enough already."

"Owen here knows the location of the cave in the Macgillycuddy Mountains in which the chalice is hidden. He's on our side now," Brendan said. "He saw the Dermot the Daring at his back-stabbing worst."

"That's right. Being an evil ghost is a mean and ugly business," Owen said. "That Dermot fella isn't very nice. He never keeps his word. I like the ghost folk around here much better after all. I always have."

"Come, we must be on our way. Will you be joining us, Doreen?" Brendan said.

"No. I think I'll stay here with Merlin and brew some tea for when you all return," Doreen said.

In the next instant, Danny, Melinda, Brendan and Owen were outside the narrow entrance of a cave high in the Macgillycuddy Mountains. It was pitch black. A cold wind whistled across the barren slopes.

"Follow us," Brendan said.

"Wait. Let me get my flashlight," Danny said.

While Owen and Brendan had no trouble floating through the small entrance, Danny and Melinda had to crawl on their hands and knees. The passage was particularly tight for Danny, who carried the cloth, ring, shawl and stone in his backpack.

After descending for five minutes, Danny and Melinda entered a cavern. Danny pointed his flashlight to where Owen and Brendan pointed. There on the stone floor was the Celtic chalice of Boru. It glittered in the beam of Danny's flashlight.

"Hurry, lad," Owen said. "Place the objects you gathered around the chalice."

Danny did what he was told. Nothing happened. A few more minutes went by. There was only silence. Then the cavern suddenly started to feel warmer. The chalice started glowing as if it were on fire. The floor began to shake and rocks began to fall from the ceiling.

"Cover your head, Melinda!" Danny yelled.

"It's working! It's working!" Brendan screamed.

The chalice became red hot like lava from a volcano. Then other ghosts streamed into the cavern. These were the evil ghosts who had taken over the bodies of so many people in Ireland and were doing so much harm. Even Dermot the Daring was there. The evil ghosts circled the chalice and screamed in dismay. But there was nothing they could do. The objects that Danny and Melinda had brought were too powerful. One by one, the evil ghosts began to disappear until only Dermot remained.

"You will pay for this, Owen," Dermot said menacingly as his voice and ghostly form began to grow weak and eventually fade away to nothing.

Then it was over. The Celtic chalice had melted into a small, smoldering puddle of gold. The evil ghosts were gone, banished forever to the Forest of Kenmare. On windy nights, people who lived near the forest thought that they heard the trees moaning, as if the trunks and branches and leaves were alive and in pain. They decided that they were just hearing things or that they had one too many glasses of beer or Irish whiskey.

But Danny and Melinda and all of the good ghosts knew that the desperate sounds were from the spirits of Dermot the Daring and his dark council longing to escape and regain power but knowing that their cells would never be unlocked.

Chapter 21

"You've done a magnificent job," Brendan told Danny and Melinda. "Dermot will never cause trouble anymore and give ghosts a bad name. The human leaders are now leading, the jailers are now jailing and the judges are now judging properly, as they should. Everything is back to normal, or as normal as things get around here."

"Thanks," Danny said. "But we were wondering if you would take us home now."

"Yeah," Melinda said. "We miss our parents and friends."

"I miss baseball," Danny said. "But don't get me wrong, that hurling match was really fun."

"I'm glad that you enjoyed it. It was grand indeed," Brendan said, adding: "Well, yes, I think it's time for you to return home. Enough chit-chat."

"We'll miss you and Liam and all of the ghosts we met. And we'll miss you Doreen," Danny said.

"And I'll miss you. And so will Merlin," Doreen said. "But you belong at your own home. Goodbye."

Doreen gave Danny and Melinda a big hug. "Wait, I have some gifts for ya," Doreen said. She walked quickly into her bedroom and then returned with a beautiful white sweater for Danny and a red shawl for Melinda.

"This is beautiful, Doreen, and warm," Danny said after putting on the white wool sweater. "It'll be perfect for the cold winters back in Rivertown."

"And I just love my shawl," Melinda said. She wrapped it around her shoulders and looked at herself admiringly in the mirror.

"It's just like the one my Aunt Mary used to wear," Doreen said.

"Did you make these yourself?" Melinda asked.

"That I did. That I did," Doreen replied.

"But how could you knit them so quickly?" Danny said.

"I had a little help with a magic knitting spell that I found in my book of household chore spells. It was really a time saver," Doreen explained. "Off with ya now," she then said, "before I begin to cry like an old fool."

"Doreen, don't cry. Remember that you and Brendan have some chores to do for us. We would have liked to do them ourselves, but we really want to go home now. Right, Danny?" Melinda said.

"Yeah, " Danny said. "We feel kind of bad about having you return the things we found. But we really do want to get back to Rivertown."

"So will you make sure that everything we borrowed is returned to their proper places?" Melinda said. "The sacred cloth of St. Patrick needs to be reburied near Glendalough. McGinty's ring needs to be returned to him like we promised. And you have to visit him from time to time. You need to take back the mermaid's golden shawl. She really looked sad after we took it. And then you have to put back the stone of truth."

"We won't forget, lass," Doreen said, smiling but also trying to hold back a tear. "We won't forget."

"Of course we won't forget. All right, now. We've got that all squared away to everyone's satisfaction. By my reckoning, it's nighttime back where you live, " Brendan said. "So we best go now so that I can exchange you for your doppelgängers without your parents noticing a thing. So one more time, lad and lass, touch my hand."

The next instant Danny and Melinda were back in their bedrooms in their home in Rivertown. They could tell that their doppelgängers had been sleeping in their beds because the sheets were wrinkled. But their doubles were gone.

"Danny, my boy," Brendan said. "We're in your debt. If ever we can help you with anything, let us know."

"But how can we get in touch with you?" Danny said.

"You know that old house on 4th Street? The big stone mansion that's been boarded up for years?" Brendan said.

"Yeah, the creepy old Ryan place," Danny said.

"Well, I know the ghosts that haunt the house. I'll put in a good word for ya while I'm passing through. If you want to contact me, just pay a visit to the ghosts there. Well, there you have it, lad. I must head back to the old sod—Ireland that is."

"Goodbye, Brendan," Danny said.

"Goodbye, lad," Brendan said. "And maybe you should think about taking up golf. It's a wonderful sport." And then Brendan disappeared.

In the days that followed, Danny and Melinda got back into their regular routines. Their parents noticed that the two of them had suddenly began talking louder and causing more trouble than just after they had returned from Ireland. Danny and Melinda just smiled at each other, knowing that their doppelgängers must have been quieter and better behaved than they were.

After Chip returned from baseball camp, Danny told him all about his adventure in Ireland as they sat in their treehouse near an abandoned stone quarry. Chip thought that Danny was making the whole thing up.

"I swear that I'm telling you the truth. You can ask Melinda," Danny said. "But if you really don't believe me, I dare you to come with me to the old Ryan mansion tonight when it's dark and the bats are flying through the air. We can talk to the ghosts that haunt the place."

"There are really ghosts there?" Chip said. "I just thought that people were seeing things after they had too much to drink."

"It's all true, "Danny said. "And don't believe everything you might have heard about ghosts. They can surprise you. So are you coming with me or not?"

Chip hesitated at first and then said: "OK. I guess I will. But if anything happens, you'll be in big trouble!"

"Nothing will happen. I understand the ghost world. In

fact, I guess that you could call me an expert in matters of the spirit world," Danny boasted.

Chip then asked Danny to repeat the details of every encounter that he had with the ghosts of Ireland. If Chip was going to meet ghosts, he wanted to be prepared and know how to act. Danny was happy to do it. He just loved to tell a good ghost story.

The End (An Deireadh)

ABOUT THE AUTHOR

William Graham is a graduate of Northwestern University. He and his wife Jacqueline live in Chicago, Illinois.

ABOUT GREATUNPUBLISHED.COM

www.greatunpublished.com is a website that exists to serve writers and readers, and to remove some of the commercial barriers between them. When you purchase a GreatUNpublished title, whether you order it in electronic form or in a paperback volume, the author is receiving a majority of the post-production revenue.

A GreatUNpublished book is never out of stock, and always available, because each book is printed on-demand, as it is ordered.

A portion of the site's share of profits is channeled into literacy programs.

So by purchasing this title from GreatUNpublished, you are helping to revolutionize the publishing industry for the benefit of writers and readers.

And for this we thank you.